by Molly Reisner

Grosset & Dunlap
An Imprint of Penguin Group (USA) Inc.

© 2010 Viacom International Inc. Madagascar ® DWA L.L.C. All Rights Reserved. Used under license by Penguin Young Readers Group. Published by Grosset & Dunlap, a division of Penguin Young Readers Group, 345 Hudson Street, New York, New York 10014. GROSSET & DUNLAP is a trademark of Penguin Group (USA) Inc. Printed in the U.S.A.

Library of Congress Control Number: 2009041744

ISBN 978-0-448-45261-6          10 9 8 7 6 5 4 3 2 1

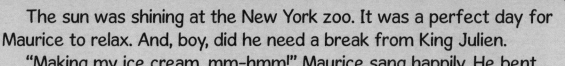

The sun was shining at the New York zoo. It was a perfect day for Maurice to relax. And, boy, did he need a break from King Julien.

"Making my ice cream, mm-hmm!" Maurice sang happily. He bent down to grab a cherry for his ice-cream sundae. But when he popped back up, his sundae was gone. King Julien had eaten it!

"Less sprinkles next time," the king said.

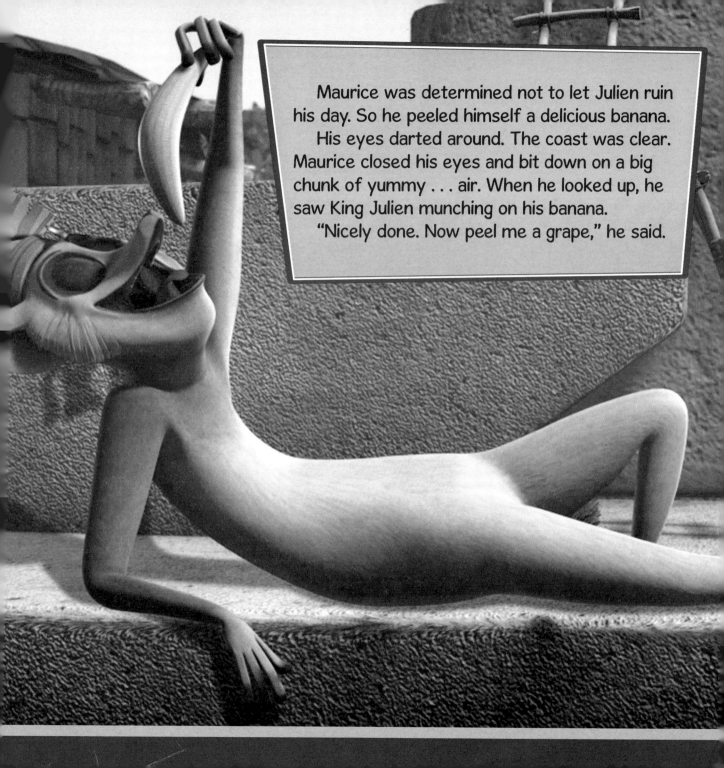

Maurice was determined not to let Julien ruin his day. So he peeled himself a delicious banana.

His eyes darted around. The coast was clear. Maurice closed his eyes and bit down on a big chunk of yummy . . . air. When he looked up, he saw King Julien munching on his banana.

"Nicely done. Now peel me a grape," he said.

Nearby, the penguins kicked back in the sun with some frozen drinks.

"Private, these sardine smoothies are top-notch. What's your secret?" asked Skippe

"Love, sir. I made them with love," said Private, proud of his recipe.

This alarmed Skipper. He slapped the drinks out of everyone's wings. "No more love in the smoothies!" he barked. "We've got to stay sharp."

Rico burped, possibly in agreement. It was hard to tell.

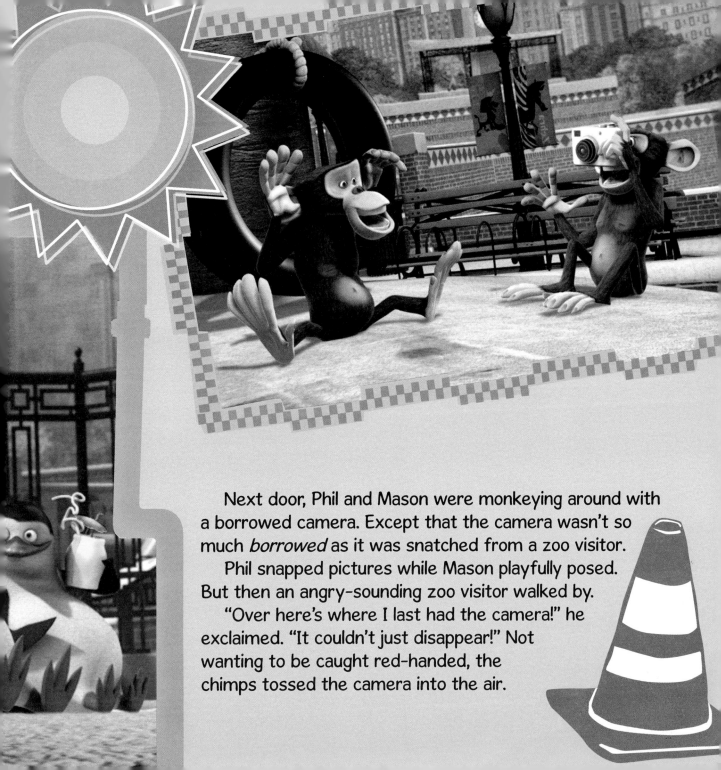

Next door, Phil and Mason were monkeying around with a borrowed camera. Except that the camera wasn't so much *borrowed* as it was snatched from a zoo visitor.

Phil snapped pictures while Mason playfully posed. But then an angry-sounding zoo visitor walked by.

"Over here's where I last had the camera!" he exclaimed. "It couldn't just disappear!" Not wanting to be caught red-handed, the chimps tossed the camera into the air.

Meanwhile, the camera flew through the air, landing in Maurice's hands. King Julien snatched the camera from Maurice. But Maurice was tired of Julien's sticky fingers.

"Gimme!" demanded King Julien, tugging at the camera. "What part of *gim* or *me* did you not understand?"

"I understood the *me* part. Like this was caught by *me*, for *me*!" Maurice yelled, pulling the camera with all his might.

During their fierce tug-of-war, King Julien accidentally pressed a button on the camera. A flash of blinding light went off. Maurice and the king tumbled in opposite directions. The camera landed with a thud.

The king sat up, feeling dazed. Maurice was nowhere to be seen.

"Maurice?" he called. "Where are you and your booty which is quite large and is usually easy to see?"

Then Mort picked up the camera. An image of Maurice was on the screen.

"He's trapped!" Mort screamed.

"Uh . . . Yes. That is what happens when you question the king's power!" King Julien said, thinking Maurice was stuck inside the camera.

Julien stared at the camera, waiting for Maurice to say something. "Oh," he said. "You are giving to me the 'silent treatment.' I also, too, can give you *the treatment!*"

The penguins walked by, witnessing Julien's fury. "Speaking to a camera. This is not normal," stated Skipper.

"Maurice questioned my kingly authority, so now he's trapped in this magic thingy which the sky spirits sent me, the king," King Julien explained.

Skipper rolled his eyes. There was no way to make the king believe the camera wasn't magical. "All right, boys. Let's leave the madman to his madness," he said.

Then Skipper felt a tiny tug on his wing. It was Mort, looking worried. "Spit it out, sad eyes," Skipper said.

"The king's giving Maurice *the treatment*," Mort whispered. "He's going to leave him in the magic box. You have to help get him out. Pleeeeeease!" Then he batted his eyelashes to look extra cute. This had no effect on Skipper.

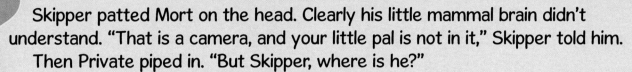

Skipper patted Mort on the head. Clearly his little mammal brain didn't understand. "That is a camera, and your little pal is not in it," Skipper told him.

Then Private piped in. "But Skipper, where is he?"

He had a point. Skipper decided to lead an investigation to find the missing lemur. "Let's crack this mystery wide open," Skipper said. "We're looking for anything that might be a clue."

Armed with a magnifying glass, Rico began to inspect his surroundings. First he found a banana peel, which he ate right away.

"Hey, mister, that's evidence," scolded Skipper. Then he peered through Rico's magnifying glass. There were lemur tracks leading off the edge of the platform!

Then Skipper took a closer look. "My guess is he stumbled backwards. But why?" he said.

Private had a theory. "Maybe the camera's flash blinded him?" he offered.

"Sounds a little preposterous, Private," said Skipper. "But just in case . . . Kowalski, run a temporarily blinded, portly lemur scenario."

Kowalski brought Rico to the edge of the platform where Maurice's footprints ended. There was only one way to find out what had happened to the lemur.

"Stand right here, Rico," Kowalski said. Then, suddenly, Kowalski pushed him off the ledge. Rico fell down, landing on the king's blow-up bouncy toy. He sprang back into the air and over the wall, landing inside a trash can!

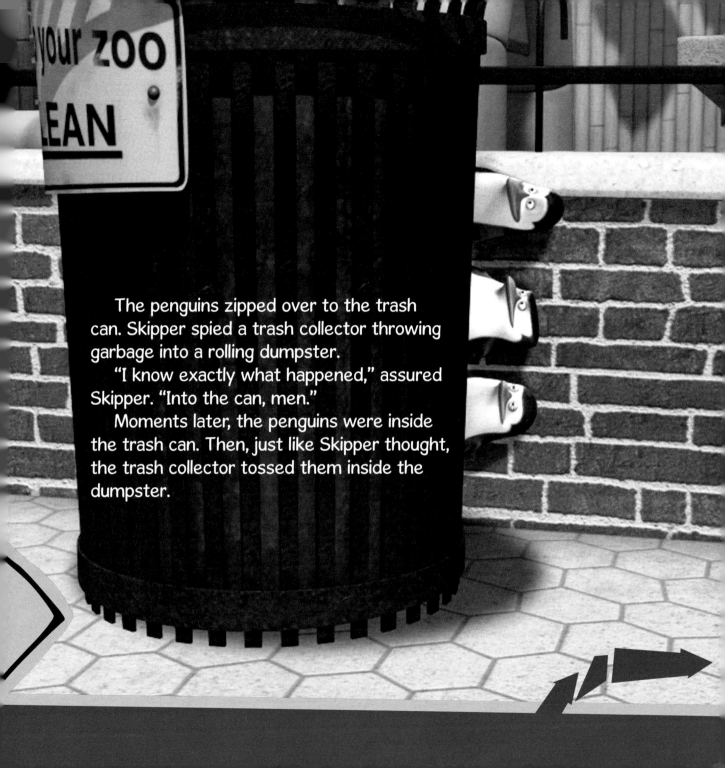

The penguins zipped over to the trash can. Skipper spied a trash collector throwing garbage into a rolling dumpster.

"I know exactly what happened," assured Skipper. "Into the can, men."

Moments later, the penguins were inside the trash can. Then, just like Skipper thought, the trash collector tossed them inside the dumpster.

Later that night, the penguins reached their destination: the dump.
Skipper sprung out of the trash heap like a jack-in-the-box.
"Kowalski, coordinates!" he barked.
"New Jersey," Kowalski answered, spotting the state's license plate.
Skipper happily inhaled a whiff of garbage. "All right, listen up," he
said. "We are going to search this dump high and low."

Then Private shouted out, "Skipper, over here!" The penguins waddled over to Private, who had already found Maurice.

"What are you doing here?" Maurice asked.

"We're here to rescue you," said Private.

Maurice shook his head. "No way. No how," said Maurice. "I have had it with Julien. He's been a royal pain in my tail for too long."

After some convincing, the penguins finally talked Maurice into going home with them. He couldn't live in a dump forever! So the penguins began to race along the open road, dodging cars on the trek back to the zoo.

"This is insane! You are insane!" Maurice yelled, trying to keep up.

The group soon approached a highway tollbooth. The penguins and Maurice needed to pay to pass through.

"Rico!" Skipper ordered.

Rico knew just what to do. On command, he coughed up the correct amount of coins so they could pass through the gate.

Then the group began walking along some empty train tracks. Maurice was lagging behind.

"Gotta . . . rest . . ." he gasped, trying to catch his breath.

"No dice," said Skipper. "We have to be back at the zoo by oh-nine-hundred hours."

"Which does not give us much time," added Kowalski.

"There's no way I can go faster!" said Maurice.

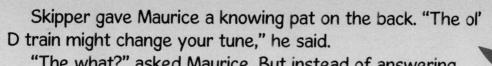

Skipper gave Maurice a knowing pat on the back. "The ol' D train might change your tune," he said.

"The what?" asked Maurice. But instead of answering him, the penguins took a running start and slid down the side rails. Maurice was left clueless until, seconds later, a bright light began to shine on the lemur. A horn wailed. A train was coming!

"Aaaaah!" screamed Maurice, running as fast as he could.

Back at the zoo, King Julien was staring at Maurice's picture.

"Stop looking at me like that!" he told the camera. "I am shutting up now because you are still getting the *shhh* treatment."

But deep down, the king missed his friend. He hugged the camera tightly.

"I can't take it anymore. You win!" he cried. "I will give anything to get my big-bootied buddy back!"

Then King Julien had a brilliant idea. He could smash the camera with a heavy rock tied to a vine. "Now we break poor Maurice out of his magical prison!" Julien announced.

Mort placed the camera underneath the rock. "A little to the left," he told Mort. Mort scratched his head. "My left or your left?" he asked innocently.

"Mine, of course!" King Julien said. "I am king. The lefts are all mine!"

Meanwhile, the penguins and Maurice were almost home. On the streets of New York City, Skipper saw a bus headed toward the zoo. The penguins tossed Maurice inside. After a short ride, Maurice stumbled down the bus steps, exhausted from the hectic journey.

"All right, boys," announced Skipper. "Commence Operation Shoot the Moon!"

The penguins put together a makeshift catapult. They wanted to fling Maurice over the zoo wall to get him back home.

Private saddled himself into the catapult for a test run. Rico pulled back on the catapult and let go. Private arced through the air and . . . *SPLAT!* He smashed into the brick wall.

"Ooof!" he yelled, sliding down the wall.

Kowalski quickly made some adjustments to the catapult. Then Skipper called Maurice over. "Lemur! You're up!" he said, slapping Maurice cheerfully on the back.

Maurice stepped backward, his whole body quaking with fear. "I can't take it anymore! You penguins are psychotic!" he yelled.

But Kowalski grabbed Maurice and plunked him down in the launch seat. Seconds later, Maurice was slicing through the air.

"Aaaaaah!" he screamed.

At the lemur habitat, King Julien was still ordering Mort to move the camera around so he could smash it to bits.

"Mort, a little more to the left," the king said.

Finally, Julien was satisfied with the camera's position. He released the vine and dropped the big rock onto the camera, and . . .

. . . *BAM!* King Julien dropped the rock directly on top of Mort.

"Eeeee!" yelled a squashed Mort.

King Julien didn't even notice that Mort was being squished. He rushed toward the camera and knelt down to talk to it. "Maurice!" he cried out. "I want you back! Great sky spirits, hear my plea!"

Just then, Maurice fell from the sky and landed on the camera's flash button.

*FLASH!* The blinding light sent King Julien reeling backward. He sat there for a second, stunned at the appearance of Maurice, who was lying on top of the camera.

"Maurice!" King Julien exclaimed.

The king scooped up his pal in a big upside-down hug. "I am so glad you are back!" King Julien exclaimed.

Maurice knew one thing for sure: Tolerating King Julien might be a big pain in his booty, but it was far better than spending one more terrifying second with those crazy penguins.

"It's good to see you, too," Maurice said, meaning every word.

In the middle of their special moment,
Skipper waddled over to the king and Maurice.
"Mission accomplished," Skipper said proudly.
The king shook his head in disbelief. "Oh, as
if you had anything to do with it. The sky spirits
released Maurice!" Then King Julien looked up,
throwing his hands in the air. "You rock, sky
spirits!" he shouted.

Skipper arched an eyebrow. "Why don't you tell the king what really happened, rescued mammal?" he said to Maurice.

But after his time spent with the penguins, Maurice knew exactly how to answer Skipper. He stuck out his chest and proudly announced, "Rule number one: Do not question the king!"